THE HANDOFF

Katherine Hengel

SADDLEBACK
EDUCATIONAL PUBLISHING

DISTRICT ⑬

SADDLEBACK
EDUCATIONAL PUBLISHING
www.sdlback.com

ISBN-13: 978-1-61651-583-6
ISBN-10: 1-61651-583-X
eBook: 978-1-61247-248-5

Printed in the Malaysia

21 20 19 18 17   6 7 8 9 10

1

Xavier sat across from his younger brother Hugo. They were alone in the subway car. It was about 10 p.m.

"No pills," Xavier said. "*Especially* from Emilio. And don't drink."

Hugo rolled his eyes. "Stop hatin' on Emilio," he said. "So he's with Clara. Get over it."

Xavier did not respond. He looked out the window. It was true. Emilio was on his last nerve. Clara was only part of it. Emilio was getting cocky. He wasn't afraid of cops anymore. He was taking too many risks.

The subway slowed down. This was their stop.

"Grab your transfer," Xavier said. "We gotta catch a bus."

"You said Freeport."

"Yeah, the other side of it," Xavier said. "Let's move. We'll take the 23."

Xavier stepped through the doors. Hugo looked on the floor. He picked up his muddy transfer. Then he followed his brother.

They hustled to the 23 stop. But they missed the bus. The 23 didn't run much at night. So they walked. They reached Emilio's an hour later.

"This way," Xavier said. "Around back."

"Where his mom at?" Hugo asked.

"Don't matter. She doesn't care what we do," Xavier said.

Xavier led Hugo between two houses. They climbed stairs to a back deck. Xavier saw his best friend Angelo.

"What up, Angelo?" Xavier said.

Angelo held out his hand. "You miss the 23?"

"That bus is jacked," Xavier said.

Angelo nodded. "Nice night though. Feels like spring. Nice lid, Hugo. Lookin' pretty fly."

"Even better than your brother!" Clara joked. She stepped onto the deck. She closed the sliding door.

Hugo blushed. "I'm going in," he said. He walked behind Clara. Then reached for the door.

"Hey, Hugo," Xavier called out.

Hugo was annoyed. "*What?*"

"Be good."

2

Xavier watched Hugo go inside. Then he leaned on the deck railing. Angelo stared at him.

"See something you like?" Xavier asked.

"Surprised you brought him," Angelo said. "That's all."

"Me too," Clara added. She had a small pipe in her hand. She passed it to Xavier.

"*Please*," Xavier snapped. "He'd come anyway. Kid wants to be here. At least I can watch him."

"He shouldn't want this," Angelo said.

Xavier took a hit. "Yeah? What should he want, Angelo?"

"I don't know. Baseball. Hell, track and field. *Something*."

Xavier smiled. "You're still fast, Angelo. Get back on the team. You got two years still."

Angelo sat quietly. "I go back when you go back," he said to Xavier.

Xavier took another hit. "My track career went up in smoke," he said.

Inside, Hugo sat on the couch. He heard Emilio in the kitchen. He felt in his pocket. Yep. He had a lighter. He tried to sit up straight. He wanted to look bigger. But the old couch was busted. He just sank lower.

"Hey! There he is!" Emilio yelled.

Hugo was all smiles. "What up, Emilio?" he said.

Emilio pulled out a fresh smoke. He put it up to his lips. Hugo stood quickly. He pulled out his lighter. He lit Emilio's smoke.

"Xavier bring you?" Emilio asked.

"Yeah."

Emilio looked surprised. He threw his arm around Hugo. He was pretty smashed. "Know what this party is for?" he slurred. "Me bangin' Clara. One month today. Should I keep her? Another month?"

Hugo didn't say anything.

"Smart!" Emilio said. He squeezed Hugo even closer. "I love this kid! Carries a lighter for me. You believe that?" Then Emilio fell into the couch.

Raul came into the room. "Ready, Emilio?" he asked.

"For what?"

"A delivery," Raul said. He lit a smoke.

"Kush?"

"Yep. An ounce," Raul replied.

Emilio nodded. "Hugo, find your brother. We got business."

Hugo left the room. Emilio barked one more order. "And tell Clara to get in here. Haven't seen her all night."

"She's on the deck," Raul said. He passed Emilio a small silver flask. "With Xavier."

Emilio unscrewed the top of the flask. He took a long pull. He yanked Raul's cigarette from him. Then he stuck it in the flask.

"What the hell, Emilio?" Raul yelled. "Why you do that?"

"Because I can," Emilio smirked.

Outside, Hugo found Xavier. He was still on the deck. So was Clara.

"Hey, Xavier, Emilio wants you. Says he has business. Um, Clara? You too."

Clara looked at Xavier. She was sad. Xavier emptied her pipe. He stood up and passed it to her. "Thank you," he said. She nodded and went inside.

Angelo stood up too. "Xavier, I wasn't playin'. Let's do it. Let's start over. Get back into it."

"What? Track?" Xavier laughed.

Angelo nodded.

"Sure, Angelo. Hell of an idea."

"You *promise*?"

Angelo wasn't playing. Xavier looked at him carefully. Hugo looked at Xavier. No one said a thing.

Finally Xavier spoke. "All right, Angelo. We'll do it. We'll start over. Get back on track."

"Word," Angelo smiled. "Get your bro home. I got this one."

"For real?"

"For real," Angelo said.

Xavier smiled. "Thanks, Angelo. *"Hasta mañana.* See ya tomorrow."

"Hasta mañana," Angelo replied.

3

The next morning, Xavier and Hugo walked to school. Hugo walked quickly. He was about ten feet ahead of Xavier.

"Why you walkin' so fast?" Xavier yelled. "Excited for class?"

"*You* excited for track?" Hugo snapped.

Xavier laughed. "Damn, Hugo. Use your head. That'll never happen."

Hugo didn't respond. He just walked faster.

"Say I did join. What's it to you?"

"No one in the gang joins track," Hugo explained. "It'd be like you quit. Quit the gang. Where's that leave me?"

"Why do you care, Hugo? Those fools are punks. Punks pretending to be drug dealers. Especially Emilio."

"Then why's Angelo scared of Emilio?" Hugo asked.

"Angelo ain't afraid of Emilio. Emilio *needs* Angelo. Just like he needs me. We're his drivers. He can't do business without us. That's why we get a piece. Understand?"

"Emilio doesn't need you," Hugo said.

"The hell he doesn't. Emilio has a record, Hugo. It's bad. Real bad. That fool will never drive again. Emilio has the place. The hub. Plus his mom's car. That's it."

"What's Raul for?" Hugo asked.

"Raul's cousin is the main man. The supplier. So he's automatically in. Raul just hangs around. Eats Emilio's crap all the time."

"What could I do?" Hugo asked. "I want in. You *know* that. How do I get in?"

Xavier didn't answer. He saw Raul running toward them.

"He's joining track too I suppose," Hugo said.

"Shut your mouth," Xavier said. "Something's wrong."

Raul caught up to them. He was breathless. "Xavier, they crashed. Last night. On the highway."

"Who, Raul? Who crashed?"

"Emilio, Clara, and Angelo. My mom told me. They came in together on her shift. She said it was bad."

"How bad?" Xavier asked.

"I don't know. Angelo got it the worst. Clara is pretty messed up too. Emilio will be okay. That's all I know."

Xavier's heart hurt. *Angelo got it the worst.*

4

Xavier, Hugo, and Raul skipped
school. They went to the hospital.
A nurse told them they couldn't see
Clara or Angelo. Just Emilio.

They entered his room slowly.
Hugo took his hat off. He wanted to
show respect.

"*Que pasa*, Emilio? What's
happening?" Raul asked. "I thought
you'd look worse."

"You hurtin'?" Xavier asked.

"Nah," Emilio grinned. "I got tiger's blood. I gotta get the hell out of here. Imagine the money we're losing! Me and Angelo stuck in here."

Xavier felt sick. "Damn, Emilio. Angelo's in a coma. I doubt he cares."

Emilio nodded. "You see him yet?"

"We can't. He's in the ICU."

"What about Clara?" Emilio asked.

"Nope. Still too bad I guess."

Emilio looked away.

"I need a minute with Emilio," Xavier said. Raul and Hugo looked at each other. Then they left the room.

"What the hell, Emilio? What happened?"

Emilio sighed. "Angelo missed the turn, Xavier. You know. The big one."

"That's just not like him," Xavier said. "Damn. I can't believe this."

"For real," Emilio said.

"I should have been driving," Xavier sighed.

"Shake that off, man. You'll get your chance."

"No way, Emilio."

"What you sayin'?"

Xavier took a deep breath. "I don't want this anymore. Not for Hugo either. I can't be in and keep him out. I gotta … I don't know. Set an example I guess. Something like that."

Emilio nodded slowly. Xavier kept talking.

"It's too messed up, Emilio. Hell. Angelo and me. Last night we talked about track, man. How we should get back into it. Who knows if he'll … be able to … I just …"

Emilio raised his eyebrows. "You want out."

"Yes," Xavier said. "I want out."

Then there was silence.

"Hell. Life is short, Xavier," Emilio finally said. "Car crashes teach you that. You do what you gotta do. Plenty of guys would kill for your slice of the pie. There are other drivers. I'll just have to find one."

A nurse entered the room. She asked Xavier to leave.

"*Hasta luego*, Emilio," Xavier said. "See ya later."

Xavier walked out of the room. He met Hugo and Raul in the hall.

"I'm out," Xavier told them. "For good. Done. Come on, Hugo. Let's go."

Xavier walked down the hall. Hugo followed him. Raul stayed at Emilio's door.

"What the hell, Xavier! Are you nuts? What did you say?" Hugo asked.

"Said I was out. Simple as that."

"What did Emilio say?"

"Said he'd find another driver. That's it. Done. Over. Finished."

They walked to the hospital bus stop. It was just across the street. Xavier stared at the windows. He imagined each room. Each person. He thought of Angelo and Clara.

"I'm gonna do it, Hugo. Track. Starting tomorrow. You in?"

"Nah. That's all you."

Xavier saw the bus. "Got your transfer?" he asked.

Hugo reached in his pocket. He had it. But he was missing something. "Damn," he said. "Left my hat up there. Be right back. We'll have to catch the next bus."

Xavier nodded. Hugo ran into the hospital.

5

Hugo ran through the hospital doors. He made his way to Emilio's room. Emilio was happy to see him.

"Miss me?" Emilio asked.

"You know it," Hugo smiled. "Forgot my hat too."

"Saw that," Emilio said.

Hugo picked up his hat. The room went quiet. Hugo felt weird. He didn't know what to say. Plus, Emilio might hate his guts. Xavier was out now. So it was hard to say.

"Bet you want a smoke, huh?" Hugo said.

Emilio laughed. "Damn straight."

Hugo smiled. Then he looked down at the floor.

"Your brother tell you? His big news?" Emilio asked.

"Yeah," Hugo said.

"Where's that put us, Hugo?" Emilio asked.

"What do you mean?"

"I'm out of here tomorrow," Emilio said. "I lost your brother today. And Angelo, well. You know. Here's the point. I got room, Hugo. I could use you. What do you say? You want in?"

"I don't have a license," Hugo gasped.

"Not what I asked you," Emilio replied. "I asked if you're *in*."

"Yes. Hell, yes. I'm in, Emilio."

6

The next morning, Xavier looked in his dresser. He was looking for track clothes. He grabbed an old T-shirt. He held up an old pair of shorts. He hadn't worn them for years. Would they still fit?

"No one wears those," Hugo said.

Xavier knew he was right.

"You're gonna look like a fool," Hugo said.

"Thanks, Hugo. Thanks a lot," Xavier said. He shoved the clothes in his bag and left.

After school, Xavier changed in the bathroom. He wasn't ready for the locker room. No way. Not yet.

He checked himself out. Damn. His shorts *were* too small. "Yep. You look like a fool," he said to himself. He thought about running home. But he didn't. He walked to the track.

Of course, everyone stared at him. "To hell with this," he thought.

Then Coach Perez blew the whistle. "Warm up! Two laps! First one at 30 percent. Next one at 60."

All Xavier heard was two laps. He just started running! He ran the first lap as fast as he could. He passed everyone! "I still got it," he thought. "Short shorts or not. I'm still fast!"

But by the second lap, he was winded. It was hard to breathe. He had no energy. Everyone passed him. "What the hell?" he thought.

Coach blew the whistle again. It was time for stations. Everyone knew where to go. Except for Xavier.

Coach met him in the center of the track. "Glad you're here," he said. "First few days will be rough. But you have speed. I remember. Don't give up. Okay, Xavier?"

Xavier nodded.

"Remember the batons? How to pass 'em?" Coach asked.

"Sort of," Xavier replied. They practiced a few handoffs together.

Xavier felt silly pretending. But Coach said he was a natural.

"It's called the exchange zone," Coach said. "It's critical. Most important part of the race. You gotta pass on something good. You owe it to your teammate. Understand?"

Xavier nodded.

"All right. Go over by Shaw. Remember him? He'll rotate you in on a relay."

Xavier did what Coach said. Shaw put him in as second runner. True, he was out of shape. But he could still handle 100 meters. And his handoffs weren't bad! He focused on the exchanges.

"Still got some legs, huh?" Shaw said.

Xavier smiled. Soon practice was over. Good thing too. He had nothing left. He walked off the track. That's when he saw Clara. She was alone in the bleachers.

Xavier ran to her. He slowed down as he got closer. Clara's face looked like mush.

The right side puffed out like a balloon. She could barely open her eye. She had stitches on her top lip. Her whole face was purple.

"Hey," he said softly.

"Hey," she replied. She kept her head down. She wouldn't look up.

"Tried to visit you yesterday. Nurse said no visitors."

Clara nodded. "Yeah. I didn't want to see anyone. Embarrassed of my face I guess. My eye was super bad yesterday. It was oozy and gross."

Xavier lowered his head. He wanted her to look at him. "Clara, I'm sure …"

"Please don't," she said.

"Okay, I won't," he replied.

The wind came up. It blew her hair onto her face. She winced in pain. She carefully pushed it back.

"Emilio told me you quit," she said. "I'm so … happy."

"Thanks, girl," Xavier smiled.

"One more thing," Clara said.

"I know, I know," Xavier joked. "You dig my shorts."

Clara wanted to smile. But she couldn't. Her face was too sore. "Angelo would be proud."

7

Xavier walked Clara to her house. Then he walked home. He felt better than he had in days. But then he saw a familiar car on his street. It belonged to Emilio. Well, his mom, actually.

He knew it from a mile a way. He had driven it all over the city. One end to the other for years. He saw Hugo get out of the back.

Xavier walked fast up to the car. "Stay right frickin' there," he said to Hugo.

"Don't you dare screw this up for me, Xavier," Hugo snarled. But he stayed put.

Xavier looked in the car window. Emilio sat shotgun, as usual. Xavier leaned in to talk.

"Nice shorts, Xavier," Emilio joked. "Little tight, aren't they?"

Raul laughed from the driver's seat. He had a cut on his lip.

"What you running with my brother?" Xavier asked.

"The usual," Emilio said. "He has to learn. Kid wants to drive."

"Yeah? Is Raul learning too?" Xavier snapped.

"There's an art to the job, Xavier," Emilio said. "You know that. It takes a while to learn. Right, Raul?"

Raul didn't look over. He just nodded.

"Who gave you that fat lip, Raul? Your teacher here?"

Raul looked away.

"At least Raul has a license," Xavier said. "You know how old Hugo is? I told you I don't want him ..."

"Get screwed, Xavier. I need people. You left me high and dry."

Xavier looked at his brother. Hugo looked ready to kill him. It was about to get worse.

"What if I come back," Xavier said. It just came out. "I come back. You leave Hugo out."

Emilio put his hand to his chin. "I won't close my door on him. But I'll keep him off deliveries."

Xavier nodded. Then he turned from the car. Raul drove away.

"What did you say?" Hugo yelled. "I mean it. What the hell did you tell Emilio?"

"I'm back in, Hugo. You're out."

"I hate you!" Hugo said. "I hate you so bad!"

"You don't get it. Damn, Hugo!" Xavier said. "You. Me. We shouldn't be here. We should be in the hospital. Don't you get that?"

"Blame the *driver* for the crash, Xavier," Hugo said. "Not Emilio."

Xavier brought his fist back. He almost did it. Hugo didn't flinch.

"I hope you have my luck," Xavier said. "Instead of Angelo's. That's all that was. Luck."

8

Xavier walked to school the next morning. He had a pounding headache.

Clara was at his locker. "Hey," she said. She was happy. But she still hid her face.

"What's up, Clara?" Xavier asked.

"I was thinking. Know that outlet store? By the storage place? They have sports clothes. You could get some gear. You know. For track. It's pretty cheap there."

Xavier sighed. "Clara, I'm back in. Back with Emilio."

Clara looked so sad. "Don't go back, Xavier. *Please*."

"I have to."

"Why?"

"I made a deal with Emilio. I go back. He leaves Hugo out. Hugo is 14, Clara. I can't have him running drugs. Emilio only cares about *drivers*," Xavier said. "If I go back, he'll have one."

"You're a fool," Clara said. "Know why Emilio tapped your brother? Because he hates you. He's wants to hurt you. Why would he want a 14-year-old driver?"

"Emilio ain't that smart, Clara. Besides. He could hurt me easy. He'd send some guys. Rough me up. Something like that. Hasn't happened yet."

Clara looked him in the eye. It was the first time since the accident. "There's only one reason your face doesn't look like mine," she said.

"What? What you getting at?"

"I made a deal with Emilio too," she said. "He hurts you. I come clean about my face."

Xavier froze. "What?"

Clara didn't flinch. "Emilio did this *before* the crash."

"Why?"

"Because I was on the deck. Because I was with you."

Xavier took a step back. "But, Raul's mom. She said you all came together."

"That's a lie. Emilio must have told Raul that. I walked to the ER myself. It took a while. You know how far that is. Damn 23 didn't come. So I walked to the train. I got to the ER when the ambulances did."

Xavier was stunned. "Did Angelo know, Clara? What Emilio did?"

"Hell, no, Xavier! Emilio told him to wait in the car. Then he came back in for me."

"Did you see who was driving? Was Emilio driving?"

"Sorry, Xavier. I didn't catch that. I had other things on my mind."

Xavier took Clara in his arms. He held her close. "I'm so sorry, Clara."

A tear ran down her sore cheek. "Emilio got scared. He asked me what I wanted to keep quiet. I said I wanted you."

She squeezed him tighter.

"I'm gonna kill that bastard. I'm gonna kill him, Clara," Xavier swore.

"No. No you are not. You'll make it worse. We can be together now. Finally. Do you want to be with me, Xavier?"

"Of course I do, Clara. You know that. "

"Then don't confront him. And *don't* go back. *Please.*"

"I won't go back … But I gotta keep Hugo out."

Clara sighed. "Can't you just talk to him."

"No way. Kid hates me."

"What are you gonna do?"

"Gonna make a phone call."

9

Xavier ran to the school office. "I'm sick as hell. For real. I'm gonna barf! I need to call home," he said. The secretary didn't buy it. But she still passed him the phone.

He stretched the cord as far as he could. He didn't want her to hear.

Then Xavier dialed Raul's cousin. The supplier. "Please pick up. Please pick up," Xavier whispered.

"Hola."

"Hola, Cristian! Es Xavier! Que pasa, tío?" Xavier said. "What's up, dude?"

"Xavier! *Cómo estás?*" Cristian said. "How are you?"

"Better than your cousin Raul. Sorry to call so early. But Emilio has lost it, man. Gave Raul a fat lip yesterday."

"Did Raul deserve it?" Cristian asked.

"No way," Xavier said. "Emilio replaced Angelo. Get this. With a 14-year-old. Raul questioned it. Emilio snapped."

"I always liked Angelo. I like you too, Xavier. But why should I care? Emilio can use whoever he wants."

"Emilio put his girl in the hospital. The *hospital*, man. Beat her *real* bad."

"Man, that's ill. Ain't right, hurtin' females," Cristian said. "But Xavier. It ain't my business."

"She will talk, Cristian. Emilio bribed her. But she'll talk sooner or later. Then the cops will check Emilio's record. Then he'll get heat. Want him holding your goods when he does?"

"So," Cristian said. "I should sell right to you. That right? Cut out Emilio, right?"

"Hell, no, man. I'm out, Cristian. Ask Raul. I got nothing to gain. Just keeping you in the know."

10

Two months passed. Spring turned
to summer. The school year was
almost over. Hugo didn't talk to
Xavier much. Until one sunny
Saturday.

"Where you goin'?'" Hugo asked.
He was wearing Xavier's old hat. He
hadn't for a long time.

"Know that outlet store? By the
storage place?" Xavier said.

"Yeah."

"Going with Clara. Then we're gonna visit Angelo. He's talking now. Sitting up too. Wanna come?"

Hugo pulled on the brim of his hat. "Hell, yeah. It's been a while since I saw him."

The two walked together slowly. "How's business?" Xavier asked.

"There ain't any," Hugo replied.

"Sorry, bro," Xavier said.

"Emilio says it will turn. How's Clara?" Hugo asked.

Xavier smiled. "Good. Real good. She's cool as hell."

"Her face looks better," Hugo said. "Everyone says Emilio did it. You hear that?"

Xavier nodded.

"Couple guys beat him down last week. 'Cause of Clara."

"Yeah? Bad?"

"Oh yeah. *Bad*. His face is jacked. You know who did it?"

"Who?" Xavier asked.

"Quit playin'. You set it up. Didn't you?" Hugo asked.

Xavier shook his head.

"Right," Hugo said. "You're too busy. With track and all. Too busy to set up a beat down."

Xavier kept walking.

"How is track?" Hugo asked.

"It's all right. Working on handoffs still."

"Say what?"

"Handoffs? When you pass the baton? To your teammate?"

"What's so hard about that?"

"You gotta do it just right."

"Word. So he's got a good chance. So he doesn't lose speed, right?"

"Exactly," Xavier said.

"You get new shorts yet?" Hugo joked. "Tell me you got new shorts. Please."

"That's why we're going to the outlet," Xavier replied.